ELLie
ULTRA

Raintree is an imprint of Capstone Global Library Limited, a company incorporated in England and Wales having its registered office at 264 Banbury Road, Oxford, OX2 7DY – Registered company number: 6695582

www.raintree.co.uk
myorders@raintree.co.uk

Editor: Alison Deering
Designer: Hilary Wacholz

ISBN 978-1-84421-749-6 (paperback)
20 19 18 17 16
10 9 8 7 6 5 4 3 2 1

British Library Cataloguing in Publication Data
A full catalogue record for this book is available from the British Library.

Printed and bound in China.

Queen of the Spelling Bee

written by Gina Bellisario

illustrated by Jessika von Innerebner

raintree

a Capstone company — publishers for children

CONTENTS

CHAPTER 1

Queen Ellie

It was just another day in the city of Winkopolis.
Bees buzzed. Kids crawled. Daddies chuckled.
Everyone was busy doing the same old ordinary
things. Everyone, mind you, but the girl who lived
at 8 Louise Lane.

That girl was Ellie Ultra. At Winkopolis
Elementary School, she was busy writing down

facts about bees quicker than a hummingbird in a rocket-powered racecar. It was *extra*ordinary.

"Bees have two antennae, six legs and two pairs of wings," Ellie's friend Hannah read off the computer. "Their wings beat two hundred times every second. That's why bees go *bzzz*."

As part of Friday's science activity, their teacher, Miss Little, had brought the third graders to the library. They were doing a web quest to learn about the buzzy bugs.

"Got it!" Ellie exclaimed, writing everything on their worksheet. She wrote so quickly her pencil started to smoke, so she blew out the tip.

"Wow! You wrote that fast!" Hannah said with a smile. "Your pencil was on fire – literally!"

Ellie smiled too. Her superpowers came in handy at school. Hannah never minded when Ellie used them. She had even seen Ellie save their

class from slobbery alien blobs. Hannah wasn't a superhero, but she was a super friend.

As her pencil cooled off, Ellie scanned the paper. "The next quest question is: *What do bees make?*"

"Honey, of course," Hannah answered. "The website says beeswax too."

"Earwax?" Dex, one of their classmates, interrupted. He poked his nose between them. "Ewww!"

Ellie glared at Dex. She might have been the only superhero in third grade, but she still had an archenemy – Dex Diggs. Dex was a regular kid, but he was *super* annoying. Ellie was sure he was secretly an evil mastermind.

When they'd first met, Dex had made a rotten pineapple face. When Ellie had accidentally kicked a hole in the football net during PE class, Dex had called her "Super Blooper". He never stopped being mean, even after Ellie had rescued him from becoming a space pet.

"Mind your own beeswax, Dex," Hannah replied.

But Dex hovered around like a pesky mosquito until Miss Little shooed him back to his seat. Then she made her way to the front of the class.

"Girls and boys, you are doing a bee-utiful job of finding bee facts," Miss Little said. "Before you continue, Ms Bumble wants to talk to you about a different kind of bee – the Winkopolis Elementary School Spelling Bee!"

Ellie perked up. The spelling bee was less than two weeks away! Ellie couldn't wait. After all, she was a superhero – she was sure she'd be a super speller too! And with her super skills, she'd definitely win first place. After all, she could spell *trouble* – T-R-O-U-B-L-E. And she could spell *villain* – D-E-X.

Ms Bumble, the substitute librarian, came out from behind the checkout desk. She was filling in for the regular librarian, Mr Soto, who'd had to go out of town suddenly.

Ellie watched as Ms Bumble smoothed her sweater. It was black and yellow and fuzzy all over. The sweater should've made her look warm and cuddly. But something about her seemed as prickly as the Porcupine, one of Winkopolis's super-villains.

As Ms Bumble spoke, her dark eyes darted left and right. "Only the top three people from each classroom will compete in the spelling bee. You will try out on Monday, so study your list of *wordzzz!*"

With that, the substitute skittered away. The thin hairpins on top of her head twitched as she went.

"*Wordzzz?*" Ellie repeated. Maybe Ms Bumble had something caught in her throat.

Hannah spun around. "Did you hear that? We only have two more days! Have you been studying the word list?"

"Sort of," Ellie replied. She had looked at the list last Friday when Miss Little had handed it out. "What about you?"

"Yes!" Hannah squealed. "I really want to get into the spelling bee. Whoever wins practically rules the school." She gazed off dreamily. "What if I was Spelling Bee Queen?"

"That would be great." Ellie was trying to stay friendly. But who was Hannah kidding? Nobody could beat Queen Ellie, leader of L-E-T-T-E-R-S.

Ellie imagined herself on a throne made of ABCs. She'd eat alphabet soup and spell out commands.

Suddenly, Hannah let out a noisy sigh. Ellie's daydream went P-O-O-F.

Hannah grabbed her hair and started plaiting nervously. "I probably won't win though," she said. "I'm not a very good speller . . ."

"Attention, students!" Miss Little said before Ellie could reply. "I'd like to give you the answer to question eight on your worksheet. Let's call it a free-*bee*." She laughed to herself.

Everyone leaned forward, pencils at the ready.

"The question is: *Which animal is a bee's predator?* Here's a hint – the animal is our school mascot."

It's a badger! Ellie thought. She'd known that ever since School Spirit Day. Miss Little had brought in a badger puppet, which the class had named Fuzzball. In the hall, there was also a banner that read *Winkopolis Elementary School – Home of the Badgers!* hanging proudly across the stage.

"And the answer is . . ." Miss Little opened her teacher's bag and pulled out a furry animal with a striped face. "A badger!"

The whole class gasped, then burst into laughs and hollers. Ellie giggled. Using her X-ray vision, she could see that it wasn't a real badger. Miss Little was holding Fuzzball!

Just then, Ms Bumble zipped around the bookshelf. One look at the badger puppet, and she stopped dead in her tracks. Her eyes bulged. Her sweater puffed. Her hairpins stood on end.

Bzzz! The substitute flew out of sight, straight into Mr Soto's office.

Miss Little scratched her head. "I wonder why Ms Bumble had to leave so quickly," she said. Everybody just shrugged.

"She's as busy as a bee!" Owen joked. He cracked himself up and snorted.

Again, the room exploded into laughter.

"All right, class," Miss Little said, putting Fuzzball away. "Let's settle down and get back to work."

As everyone got quiet, Ellie's brain buzzed. Why had Ms Bumble been so spooked? Ellie shook her head. Who knew? Sometimes, grownups were cuckoo bananas.

Suddenly, Hannah lit up. "Hey, I have an idea!" she said. "Do you want to come over this weekend? We could study the spelling words together. What do you say, partner?"

Ellie thought about it for a minute. She always had a great time at Hannah's. They had fun putting sparkles on their nails and snacking on fancy finger foods. But studying spelling words? That sounded B-O-R-I-N-G.

"I don't know . . . I don't really feel like studying," Ellie replied.

Hannah frowned. "Oh, okay." She turned back to the computer and started plaiting her hair again.

On her imaginary throne, Ellie sank a little. She felt guilty about saying no. But why would she need to study? She was going to rule the contest.

CHAPTER 2

Royally unfair

Ellie had a super weekend. It was *really* super, in fact. On Saturday, she rescued the neighbour's dog. It was howling for help after getting stuck in the other neighbour's cat door, so Ellie freed the dog with a mighty push. The neighbour baked cookies as a thank you, but Ellie had to save them until after dinner. Even superheroes didn't get to eat dessert first.

On Sunday, Ellie rode a comet around the galaxy. The ride got a little too bumpy, especially when a meteor shower struck near Mars. So she flew back down to Earth and headed to the new park near her house.

"Wheeee!" Ellie squealed, her cape sailing above the swing set. This was way better than practising spelling. Hannah didn't know what she was missing!

* * *

On Monday morning, Ellie breezed into Room #128. The whole class was buzzing with excitement. Ellie hopped quietly into her seat. It was the day of spelling bee tryouts, and Queen Ellie, her royal word-ness, was ready.

"Listen up, spellers!" Miss Little said after morning announcements. "It's time for tryouts. Please put away your word list and line up along the whiteboard."

Lists disappeared, and kids scrambled into place. Ellie glided behind everybody else and stepped up to the end of the line.

Towards the front of the line, Hannah waved. "Good luck, Ellie!" she called, nervously plaiting her hair.

"Thanks," Ellie replied. It was just like Hannah to wish her luck. But who needed luck when you had talent?

Tryouts got into full swing. Joshua spelled his first word – *baseball* – and hit a home run. Next, Dex spelled *clock* in no time. Amanda, Payton and Owen went one after the other and – A-B-C, X-Y-Z – all got their words correct.

As Amanda high-fived Payton, Ellie scrunched her eyebrows. Everybody seemed to be a super speller. She began to worry, and then . . .

HIC! Ellie hiccupped.

The whole line of spellers turned and stared at her. Ellie tried to stay calm, but she couldn't stop *hic-hic-hiccupping.* Her hiccups packed a punch, but she knew how to thwart them.

Ellie raised her hand. "Miss Little, may I get a drink of water?"

Miss Little looked up from her word list and nodded.

Ellie zoomed out of the room, hiccupping all the way. *Hic-hic-hic!* At the drinking fountain, she took a long drink of water.

Take that, horrible hic-hic-hiccups! she thought. She waited to see if her plan worked.

Hic! Foiled! Ellie held her breath and took a bigger sip.

Hic! Double foiled!

Ellie's stomach flip-flopped. Any second now, it would be her turn to spell a word. But how could she spell anything with her hiccups getting in the way? She had to try something foolproof.

Ellie held her breath, pinched her nose, crossed her fingers and stuck her mouth under the tap. One supersized gulp later, she exhaled and wiped the drips away with her sleeve. Then she waited.

Hic!

Noooo! Ellie thought. This couldn't be happening!

Just then, Miss Little popped her head into the hallway. "Come back inside, Ellie. You're next."

It was no use. The hiccups weren't going anywhere – except back to the spelling bee tryouts with Ellie.

Ellie dragged her feet into the classroom, and Hannah came bouncing over. "I got my first word right!" she exclaimed. "It was *climb*. C-L-I-M-B!"

How could Hannah be happy? The horrible hic-hic-hiccups were on the attack, and Ellie was no match for them! She trudged to the front of the line, with guess-what tagging along – *hic-hic-hic!*

Miss Little glanced down at the word list and then up at Ellie. "Ellie, please spell *friend*."

Friend! Ellie knew that word, didn't she? She couldn't remember. If only she had studied! She gave it her best try. "*Friend – hic –* F-I-E-N-D. *Friend – hic!*"

"I'm sorry, that was incorrect," Miss Little said. "However, you did a very nice job of spelling *fiend*. Please sit down."

Ellie couldn't believe it. She was out with a capital O-U-T. And on her very first word, no less! Not only that, she had spelled *fiend*, which meant the opposite of *friend*! Ellie hung her head and slunk to her seat.

Eventually, more kids spelled words incorrectly and had to sit down. Owen spelled *Tuesday* but forgot the *e*. Amanda spelled *diner* instead of *dinner*.

It made no difference to Ellie. All she could think about was *not* being in the spelling bee. The trophy – *her* trophy – would go to somebody else. That somebody would sit on her throne and wear her crown and rule her school. It was royally unfair!

"Great job, everyone!" Miss Little announced at the end of tryouts. "And, congratulations to our top three spellers. Next week, they will compete in the school spelling bee. Let's give a hand to Payton, Hannah and . . . Dex!"

Dex? Ellie's eyes nearly popped out as the rest of the class clapped. For the first time in her superhero life, a villain had beaten her. Ellie's face puckered like a rotten pineapple.

Dex, meanwhile, smiled in all his evil mastermind glory. He paraded down the row of desks, back to his seat. "*Hic-hic-hic . . . ,*" he teased, strutting proudly past Ellie.

Ellie tried to ignore him, but her super hearing picked up every H-I-C. It was so loud she didn't hear her hiccups go away.

Hannah plopped down in her desk next to Ellie's. "I can't believe I'm in the spelling bee!" she said excitedly. "I actually have a chance to win the trophy. That would be awesome, don't you think?"

"Sure," Ellie replied quietly. She wanted to sound as happy as Hannah, but losing had put her in a heated huff. And, as if losing wasn't bad enough, Dex's teasing had made her feel extra hot.

For the rest of the day, Hannah was abuzz. She talked and talked and talked about the spelling bee. Dex, on the other hand, kept hiccupping on purpose. "*Hic-hic-hic . . . ,*" he taunted Ellie.

Ellie wished her ears had an off switch. All this spelling bee talk really stung!

CHAPTER 3

Brain pain

When Ellie got home, her ears stopped buzzing and started chirping. A loud, birdlike song – to the tune of a hundred squawking parrots – struck as she floated into the kitchen.

CHIRRRP! CHIRRRP!

"Yeeowch!" Ellie cried. She pulled her cape over her head and took cover from the awful singing.

After a moment, she X-rayed the room, on the lookout for the evil villain named Birdbrain. Sometimes, Birdbrain flew through Winkopolis, pestering people with his pain-in-the-brain music. He also dropped poop bombs, which landed in the worst places possible.

Thankfully, Ellie's X-ray scan turned up nothing more than toaster crumbs and a wrinkled blueberry.

If it isn't a villain making that racket, it's probably Mum and Dad, Ellie thought. Her parents were inventors for B.R.A.I.N., a villain-fighting superhero group. They were always busy building something. They were super genius scientists, after all.

Ellie followed the noise to their laboratory downstairs. Gadgets sat along the wall. There was the Ultra Eraser, which could wipe away spilled grape juice. Next to that was the Ultra Weather Machine. It could make the weather snowy, rainy, cloudy or sunny.

Ellie looked into the Ultra Real-Me Mirror, which showed who somebody really was. She frowned at her reflection. Just as she guessed, she saw a superhero – not a spelling bee champ.

"Hi, Ellie!" Two super genius scientists popped up in the mirror.

Ellie turned to face Mum and Dad. "I heard a noise. It wasn't Birdbrain, was it?"

"Nope, he's a jailbird," Mum answered. "I think you heard this." She grabbed a silver whistle off her desk. "It's our latest invention for B.R.A.I.N. We're calling it the Ultra Dog Trainer."

Ellie plugged her ears as Mum blew into the mouthpiece. *CHIRRRP!* The noise was L-O-U-D. *Loud.*

"Why do you need to train a dog?" Ellie asked after the noise stopped. "We don't have one, and Cyclops already knows how to do lots of stuff. See?"

She pointed to the Ultras' giant, one-eyed iguana. He was currently sitting on his rock, knitting.

"It'll help stop a new evil villain, Dr Drool," Mum explained. She handed the gadget to Ellie so she could take a closer look. "That canine criminal needs to learn how to behave."

Ellie studied the Ultra Dog Trainer. If it could train a villain like Dr Drool, maybe it could teach Dex some manners. "Will it work on an eight-year-old evil mastermind?" she asked hopefully.

Mum smiled and shook her head. "Sorry. Property of B.R.A.I.N. – not for use at school."

"Speaking of school," Dad said, closing his clipboard, "how did spelling bee tryouts go? Did you have to spell *deoxyribonucleic acid*? That's spelled D-N-A, for short."

Ellie crinkled her forehead. For somebody who knew everything about everything – even the formula for anti-gravity trainers – her dad didn't know much about third grade.

"I spelled *friend*," she said, "but I got the word wrong. It was my hiccups' fault."

Ellie's parents looked confused. "Hiccups?" Dad asked.

Ellie nodded. "But not just any hiccups – the horrible hic-hic-hiccups! They mucked up my mind. Bopped my brain. Squashed my skull. I couldn't spell anything with them getting in the way!"

Mum put her arm around Ellie. "It's okay to make a mistake, but I'm not sure you should blame your hiccups. Did you take time to study?"

"No," Ellie said. "I'm a super speller. I didn't think I needed to study."

"What *did* you do?" Dad asked.

"Hmm . . . ," Ellie said. She used her brainpower to think back on the weekend. "I saved a dog and rode a comet. And I went to the new park. The swings were awesome!"

Mum sighed. "*If* you'd studied, do you think it would've helped? Even against the horrible hiccups?"

Ellie had to admit that studying usually strengthened her spelling power. "I guess," she replied. She kicked at an anti-gravity lunchbox floating by. Foiled times four! For a super good kid, she was having a bad day.

"Well," Dad said, "I have news that'll help your mood. Comic Book Day is this Saturday at Winkopolis Books & Toys. Do you want to go?"

Like the Ultra Eraser on a grass stain, the news erased Ellie's spelling funk. Comic Book Day spelled *F-U-N*! The local shop went comic book crazy. There were superhero games and giveaways. Plus, kids came dressed as their favourite characters. It was Ellie's cuckoo-for-comic-books dream.

"Yeah!" she shouted. "Can I get the new Princess Power: Protector of Sparkle Kingdom? It's called *The Staff and the Spell*. The librarian at school said the Troll King puts Sparkle Kingdom under a nasty spell, all with a magic staff. He said it's amazing. Please, please, please, *please*?"

Dad laughed. "Sure, why not."

"Thank you, thank you, thank you, *thank you!*" Ellie exclaimed.

She flew up and twirled in mid-air. She had every Princess Power comic on the planet: *Tea Party Trolls*, *Dress of Doom* and even *The Crystal Crown*. Each one gave her bad-guy-busting ideas.

"If you'd like, you can bring a friend," Mum added. "How about Hannah? You two get along so nicely. Like peanut butter and radioactive jelly."

Ellie nodded. Hannah wasn't as cuckoo for comics as she was, but they'd still have lots of F-U-N.

Before heading upstairs, Ellie gave back the Ultra Dog Trainer. "Can you make the dog thingy not so super loud?" she asked her parents. "I have to do homework. The noise makes it hard to think. And talk. And breathe."

Dad took a pair of headphones out of his pocket. He walked over and dropped them in Ellie's hand. "Here, you can have these. They're called Ultra Sound Stoppers. They can block out any noise – bells, sirens, buzzers, you name it. And, in case you *only* want to tune out a villain, turn this dial." He pointed to a dial that said *Villain Volume Control*.

Villain Volume Control? Ellie thought. That gave her an idea. She could use the Ultra Sound Stoppers at school and tune out a certain evil mastermind. For good!

"Great!" she said. "Thanks, Dad!"

With that, Ellie flew upstairs, quick as a comet. In her room, she plugged her ears with the Ultra Sound

Stoppers. An ambulance blared. An ice cream van jingled. A marching band banged, tooted and rat-a-tat-tatted.

Ellie heard nothing.

The silence was music to her super sensitive ears. She finished her homework in peace. Then she stuffed everything into her backpack, including the Ultra Sound Stoppers.

More like Ultra Dex *Stoppers,* Ellie thought, zipping them in firmly.

CHAPTER 4

Sweetumzzz

When she arrived at school the next morning, Ellie ran into Dex's up-to-no-good grin first thing.

"Baaah!" she muttered under her breath. "Why are evil masterminds so . . . evil?"

To find out what her archenemy had planned, Ellie decided to read his mind. A-ha! It was a fake hic-hic-hiccups attack! Dex had got into the spelling bee, and he would stop at nothing to rub it in Ellie's face.

Luckily, Ellie knew just how to thwart him. She plugged her ears with the Ultra Sound Stoppers. Then she adjusted the Villain Volume Control, turning the dial all the way down.

Sure enough, after morning announcements, Dex's phoney hiccupping began. He hiccupped through a film about sea animals, break and rollerblading in PE class.

But Ellie heard not one single H-I-C. Her idea to use the Ultra *Dex* Stoppers was genius! Super genius!

With Dex under control, Ellie could take her mind off the spelling bee. During library time, she sat at a no-fake-hiccups-allowed table. There she flipped through the comic book *Ice Boy and the Deep Freeze*.

As Ice Boy snowboarded down the Sled Hill of Horror, something whooshed past Ellie. She lowered the comic and looked around.

Joshua and Owen were searching for Spy Fly books. Payton was showing Amanda a picture in *Football Girl Magazine*. Dex was sitting with Miss Little and Fuzzball. He was in trouble for peeking at Hannah's computer password.

Everything seemed okay . . . until Ellie noticed Ms Bumble.

The substitute was skittering through the library. In front of her she pushed a book cart stacked with honey jars – lots and *lots* of honey jars. As Ellie watched, Ms Bumble unloaded the cart at the checkout desk.

Grownups sure are cuckoo bananas, Ellie thought. She knew grownups liked honey with tea or toast. Her dad even squeezed some on his grapple, a snack he'd made by crossing an apple and grape's DNA. But where on earth had Ms Bumble got so much honey?

Just then, Hannah plopped down in the chair next to her. The sound made Ellie's thoughts scatter like bees around a honey-hungry bear.

"I'm so mad at Dex!" Hannah said. "He opened my notebook to look at my password. Now I have to change it before he tells the whole world! It was the perfect password too – KitKat!"

Talk about cuckoo bananas! Hannah was completely crazy about KitKat, a character from her favourite comic book series, Dance Cat Academy. Just like Hannah, KitKat loved to dance and always seemed to be getting ready for a big performance.

That reminded Ellie – she needed to ask Hannah about Comic Book Day. "I have great news!" she started. "There's this exciting thing coming up, and I was wondering if you wanted to –"

"I know!" Hannah interrupted. "There are only six days left until the spelling bee!"

Ellie frowned. She didn't want to talk about the B-E-E. Hoping Hannah wouldn't go on about it, she tried to change the subject.

"No, not that," said said. "I'm talking about Comic Book –"

"I can't wait!" Hannah blurted out. "The whole school is coming to watch since it's going to be in the hall. The whole school! That's like a jillion people, I think."

Ellie's super brain did some quick maths. It was actually four hundred and two, give or take a lunchroom helper.

"That's great," she started to say, "but –"

"Ms Bumble told me students will sit on the stage," Hannah continued. "We even get a number. That way, we'll know how to line up. I got lucky number seven!"

Hannah went on and on about the spelling bee, but Ellie stopped listening. She didn't want to hear about how Hannah was going to sit onstage with her very own lucky number. Meanwhile unlucky Ellie would be stuck in the audience doing nothing. Talk about B-O-R-I-N-G!

Ellie wondered if, maybe, just maybe, she could swap places with Hannah. It would be easy with the Ultra Body Swapperoo.

Hannah dug into her backpack and pulled out a piece of paper. "Ms Bumble also made a new word list. She said it's a special one, just for this year's spelling bee. Look!"

Ellie leaned over and read the words:

zone

zipper

zebu

zigzag

zinc

Her eyes narrowed as she skimmed the page. Every single word started with the letter *z*!

Ms Bumble's list is C-U-C-K-O-O, Ellie thought to herself.

"Will you help me practise?" Hannah asked hopefully. "I need to study all this week. With your help, I'll zip through the words. Hey! *Zip* is one of the spelling words. I've already got that one down. Z-I-P!"

"Well . . . ," Ellie said quietly. She really didn't feel like helping. In fact, she'd rather battle evil villains. Even that would be better than listening to Hannah's bee-bragging.

Still, Hannah was her *friend.* "Okay," Ellie finally said.

"Twirl-errific!" Hannah said, sounding like KitKat. She spun over to the bookshelf and returned with *KitKat: Stage Cat-astrophe.*

Ellie got back to reading *Ice Boy*. Asking Hannah to Comic Book Day would just have to wait.

Bzzz! Bzzz! Suddenly, a pair of bees buzzed past Ellie's table. They sailed through the air and landed on the checkout desk.

"Hello, *Sweetumzzz*," Ms Bumble greeted the insects. Reaching down, she gently stroked their wings.

Ellie watched as the substitute librarian petted the bees as if they were pets. It wasn't just that Ms Bumble liked honey – she was acting like a Cuckoo-for-Bees Queen!

Just then Miss Little approached the desk and scared off the bees. "Excuse me, Ms Bumble?" she said. "Can you help one of my students change her computer password? There was a slight problem, and she needs a new one."

"A problem?" Ms Bumble asked.

"Yes – oh, that reminds me!" Miss Little said. She reached into her teacher's bag. "About the other day, I'm sorry if I surprised you with the badger –"

"Did you say *badger*?" Ms Bumble interrupted, freezing up.

"Yes, but don't worry." Miss Little took out Fuzzball. "It's only a –"

"BADGER!" Ms Bumble's hairpins twitched in all directions. She skittered around the desk and made a beeline for Mr Soto's office. A moment later, the door slammed behind her.

Ellie held in a giggle. Frightened? By a badger puppet? If only it was that easy to scare off a villain!

CHAPTER 5

E–N–O–U–G–H

Over the next few days, Ellie helped Hannah study her spelling bee words.

On Wednesday, after the Rollerblade relay in PE class, she listened as Hannah spelled *zany*, *zinnia* and *zag*. In between forkfuls of extra-cheesy mac and cheese at lunch, she heard *zig* and *zoom*.

During language arts on Thursday, they wrote a noun story. Hannah spelled out her suggestions.

"Let's make our story about a Z-E-B-R-A," she said, glancing at her word list.

Ellie jotted *zebra* on their brainstorm worksheet. "Okay."

"Who goes to Planet Z-O-N-K," Hannah continued.

"Uh-huh."

"And meets a Z-O-M-B-I-E that eats brains. Oops! Not brains. I mean the zombie eats baked Z-I-T-I."

Ellie sighed and put her pencil down. "Do you want to write the story?"

"Sure!" Hannah picked up Ellie's pencil. On the worksheet, she scribbled the words *zoo, zip* and *zillion.* Then she had Ellie check her spelling.

"Everything looks good," Ellie said, barely scanning the page. She already had words coming out of her ears.

When it was time to share stories, Hannah's hand shot up into the air.

"Go ahead, Hannah," Miss Little said.

Hannah stood up and cleared her throat. "*Zach* the *zebra* lived at the *zoo*. One day, he was bored. He built a spaceship and flew to Planet *Zonk*. There Zach met a *zombie*, but the zombie didn't eat Zach's brains. The zombie's favourite food was baked *ziti*! Zach loved croissants, so they went to a French restaurant called *Zee* Place for Croissants. They ordered one *zillion* – with chocolate milk. The end."

The class clapped, and Hannah bowed. As Ellie crossed her arms, Dex leaned over and whispered, "Then Zach hiccupped all the way back to the Z-O-O. *Hic-hic-hic* . . ."

Ellie glared at him and put in her Ultra Sound Stoppers to tune him out. She could still hear everything else, including Hannah telling a new story about Zeke the *zucchini*. But at least Dex sounded a zillion miles away.

* * *

On Friday, Ellie listened to Hannah spell the last few words. Then the bell rang for break.

"Ahhh, no more spelling words," Ellie said with a relieved sigh. "Zip. Zero. ZILCH." She went to her locker to grab her cape before heading outside.

A moment later, Hannah bounced up to Ellie's locker. "Guess what! Mr Cleveland is having a pizza party for spelling bee contestants. It's in the headmaster's office. How cool is that?"

Ellie's forehead wrinkled. "A pizza party?"

"Yeah!" Hannah said. "I hear the office went bee-bonkers with decorations. It's going to be so fun!"

Just then Payton rushed over. "Let's go, Hannah! The party's starting, and I don't want to miss a thing!"

"See you after break!" Hannah said to Ellie. She skipped off and disappeared with Payton.

Ellie stayed quiet. She could not say a single *word*. Not even a L-E-T-T-E-R. Unlucky Ellie was missing out on a super-cool pizza party with Mr Cleveland. She let out a frustrated sigh and swatted at some bees flying past. How had those got into the school?

"My *sweetumzzz!*" a frightened voice buzzed. From around the corner, Ms Bumble came skittering. She pointed an angry finger at Ellie. "Be nice!" she hissed, her eyes bulging like big black balloons.

Ellie stared at Ms Bumble's eyes, and a shiver went up her spine. Each one looked like a honeycomb that was made of hundreds of smaller eyes.

Super weird, Ellie thought. She blinked. Had her super sight gone haywire? She blinked once more, but when she opened her eyes again, Ms Bumble was gone.

* * *

Ellie thought about Ms Bumble all through break. Even during silent reading time, she couldn't seem to get the substitute's strange eyes out of her mind.

She had seen the same kind of eyes in the library the previous week. Before the Buzz on Bees web quest, Miss Little had shown a drawing of a bee's eye. It had looked like a mosaic, with lots of little hexagons that were interconnected. If Ms Bumble's eyes were the same as the drawing, it meant Ms Bumble was a –

"*Psssst!* Ellie!" Hannah whispered and waved her arms from the next row, trying to get Ellie's attention.

Ellie lowered her Maximum Mouse comic book, which was her silent-reading choice, and looked over at Hannah.

"I have to tell you about the spelling bee pizza party!" Hannah whispered loudly. She put down *KitKat: The Prrrfect Role*.

"Um, maybe you should wait," Ellie said, sinking behind her comic book. After all, silent reading was supposed to be *silent*. And besides, who wanted to hear Hannah bee-brag about cheese and pepperoni?

Hannah leaned closer, ignoring Ellie's suggestion. "First of all, the pizza was awesome. It was from I Heart Pizza. I ate almost three slices. Oh, and Mr Cleveland served everybody. He was wearing a chef's hat and apron!"

The headmaster? In a chef's hat? Ellie had only seen Mr Cleveland in a shirt and tie. "Wow," she said, trying to sound interested.

"Of course there were lots of bee things," Hannah continued. "Bee napkins; black-and-yellow cups; fuzzy pom-pom bees with googly eyes. And Layla in

Mr Washington's class even told a spelling bee joke. What insect can be spelled with just one letter? A bee! Get it? B, not B-E-E!"

Ellie got it, all right. Hannah had tons of F-U-N. Wait a second – that reminded her of something. She knew where she and Hannah could have F-U-N. Together!

"Do you want to come to Comic Book Day tomorrow?" Ellie asked. "It'll be a blast! You get bookmarks and posters, and there are games like Stick the Cape on the Superhero. It's at Winkopolis Books & Toys."

"Really? They have KitKat charm bracelets!" Hannah said. "The charms are adorable kitties doing leaps and spins. I've been begging my mum for one!" She suddenly paused and looked away. "But I can't go."

Ellie's heart sank. She felt like a superhero who'd lost her sidekick. "Why not?"

"I have a ballet class on Saturday and a tap recital on Sunday, and I want to fit in some extra spelling practice," Hannah said. "The bee's almost here."

Ellie could not believe her ears. She would miss out on more fun, this time with her friend. She had heard E-N-O-U-G-H about the spelling bee.

"Ever since you got into the spelling bee, it's all you want to talk about!" Ellie snapped. "I'm tired of listening to you showing off."

"Showing off? Am not!" Hannah's cheeks turned pink. "I'm just excited. Since you're my friend, I thought you'd be excited for me too. Aren't you?"

Ellie knew the answer. But something deep down inside her heavy-as-a-robo-hippo heart was stopping her from saying it. Instead, she spelled it out: "N-O."

Hannah's mouth hung open, but nothing came out. She snapped up her book and stuck her face inside. On the cover, KitKat smiled cheerfully.

Ellie scowled and pushed away *Maximum Mouse*.
How could she read one small-as-a-squeak word? She
kept hearing her fight with Hannah over and over.
The words buzzed angrily in her head. Why wouldn't
they buzz off?

CHAPTER 6

Comic book day

The next morning, Ellie picked at her super colossal breakfast of five waffles and one dozen eggs. She barely took a bite.

"Not hungry?" Dad asked her. He stopped watching the news on the Ultra TV. "It looks like that mean old Mine-O-Taur came out of his labyrinth and snatched your appetite. That villain is the worst!"

"Very funny, Dad," Ellie replied sarcastically. Everyone knew that when the Mine-O-Taur charged into town, he only took toys, French fries and Cupcake Friends pencil toppers.

Truth was, she couldn't concentrate on eating. She was too busy thinking about her fight with Hannah. It really bugged her, even more than hearing about the B-E-E.

Ellie swatted her pesky thoughts away. Today, she would let nothing sour her mood. It was Comic Book Day. She was going to have fun – with or without Hannah. YAAA-HOOOO!

After cleaning up her plate, Ellie got dressed. She put on her Princess Power cape, leotard, skirt and most importantly, her sparkly Princess Power tiara.

"The power's in YOU!" she said, mimicking Princess Power's signature saying. She had just struck her best power pose when Mum called her to go.

At the door, Mum grabbed the keys to the Ultra Car. "We'll swing by Hannah's house to pick her up, okay?"

Ellie tugged at her Princess Power wrist cuff. "Hannah's not coming. She's . . . busy."

Mum raised an eyebrow at Dad. "Oh? Is everything all right?"

"Yeah, sure," Ellie replied with a shrug. "Come on. Let's go."

When they arrived at Winkopolis Books & Toys, Ellie flew straight inside. The shop had gone comic book berserk. Posters covered the windows. In the corner, kids took pictures with a cardboard cutout. Comic books in every size, shape and superhero spandex colour were stacked as far as the super eye could see.

"Welcome to Comic Book Day!" said a shop worker. He handed her a tote bag. "Here are some free stickers and comic books."

"Thanks," Ellie replied. "You know, I'm actually the superhero Ellie Ultra. But today, you can call me Princess Power." She pointed to the Princess Power logo on her leotard.

The worker gave a cheerful wink and went back to handing out bags.

Ellie skipped to the games section first. She played Match the Superhero Superpower and Villain Beanbag Knock-Out. On Test Your Muscle Power, she stepped right up and swung the rubber mallet.

"Oops," she squeaked when the puck exploded off the tower.

After a couple rounds of Guess That Super-Villain, Ellie leaped over to the New Comics section. There, smack-dab between *Diary of a Space Dweeb* and *Rosy Robotic*, was the new Princess Power: *Protector of Sparkle Kingdom*!

"The Staff and the Spell," Ellie whispered, wide-eyed. She grabbed a copy and pulled over a stool to read.

The story was even better than what Mr Soto had described. The Troll King, Princess Power's way-bad archenemy, planned to hypnotise Sparkle Kingdom. He wanted everybody to join his evil army!

He raised a magic staff over the kingdom. Then he chanted, "Ooga-chooga-looga-lay! From now on, you will obey. Ooga-chooga-looga-lay! You will follow what I say."

Everyone fell into a trance, until . . . Power Time! Princess Power twirled into action. She snapped the staff and broke the spell!

"Ha!" Ellie flipped the comic closed. "Trolls never win."

She gathered up her tote bag and super-new comic. Then she joined Mum and Dad at the cashier's desk.

While Ellie stood in the queue, some silver bracelets dangling from a nearby rack caught her eye. She plucked one from the hook and eyed it closely.

It was decorated with dancing kitten charms

Ellie gasped. "A KitKat charm bracelet! This is what Hannah wanted! Dad!" She held up the bracelet. "Can I get this for Hannah? She *loves* KitKat! Please, please, please, *please*?"

Dad chuckled and nodded.

"Thank you, thank you, thank you!" Ellie hopped excitedly. She still felt terrible about her fight with Hannah. The charm bracelet would make the perfect peace offering.

When it was their turn to check out, Ellie plonked everything onto the desk.

"Did you have fun today?" the cashier asked.

"Yes!" Ellie squealed. "It was even more fun than wrestling a mechanical squid!"

The casher smiled, looking slightly puzzled. "That's wonderful."

*   *   *

After Ellie got home, she changed into her usual clothes. Then she dug into her tote bag and scooped out the charm bracelet.

"Mum? Can I fly to Hannah's and give her the bracelet now?" she called. "I'll be right back."

"Sure," Mum replied. "Don't forget your cape."

"Right." Ellie grabbed her cape off the coat hook. Wearing it helped her fly her fastest. In a snap, she arrived at Hannah's house.

I can't wait to surprise Hannah, she thought, ringing the doorbell. *She's going to go KitKat B-A-N-A-N-A-S.*

The door opened, and Hannah appeared. "Hi."

"Hannah! You'll never guess what I saw while I was in the queue at Comic Book Day!"

Hannah put her hand up. "Stop. I've been thinking about what you'd said. I'm in the spelling bee, and I know why you're not happy about it."

Ellie looked confused. "Why?"

Hannah's face pinched up. "It's obvious. You. Are. *Jealouzzz.*"

"*Jealouzzz?*" Ellie echoed as the door shut firmly. Hannah was sure taking the spelling bee seriously. Seriously enough to sound like Ms Bumble!

Turning away, Ellie stuffed the bracelet into her pocket, feeling upset. Maybe she had been acting jealous. Maybe she should've been happy for her friend. Now Hannah was as angry as a hornet!

CHAPTER 7

Spell T–R–O–U–B–L–E

It was hard being friends with a hornet. Ellie learned that *very* clearly the next day.

Before school, Hannah shared her tap recital pictures with everybody except Ellie. She didn't say a word all through lunch either.

Ellie was too scared to talk to Hornet Hannah. She had faced everything from an army of Kung

Fu action figures to extra-spicy salsa. But an angry friend was the worst!

That afternoon, Ellie sat next to Hannah. She had the KitKat charm bracelet in her hand and was trying to build up the courage to give it to her friend.

Before she could, Miss Little walked over to her desk. "Ellie, before we go to the hall for the spelling bee, can you return the class library books?" the teacher asked.

"Yep," Ellie replied. Running an errand might help work up her courage. She tucked the bracelet away safely.

"Would you like to use the rolling cart?" Miss Little asked.

"That's okay," Ellie said, lifting up twenty-two books in her arms "Carrying books is easy. It's much easier than lifting a getaway car, that's for sure!"

When Ellie reached the library, she floated around the checkout desk and kneeled at the drop box. In went Amanda's *Origami Animals*, then Joshua and Owen's *Spy Fly* #9 and #10.

"Of course Dex would pick *Super-Villain Tips & Tricks*," Ellie muttered. She rolled her eyes at the book he had borrowed.

As the last book fell in, a couple of bees went zipping overhead. Ms Bumble skittered after them. She zoomed past, not noticing Ellie behind the desk.

Bzzz! Bzzz! Bzzz! The three of them flew straight into Mr Soto's office.

"I have good *newzzz*, my *sweetumzzz*," Ms Bumble buzzed from inside the office. "Soon, I will carry out my *villainouzzz* plot!"

Villainouzzz plot? Ellie knew what that spelled: *T-R-O-U-B-L-E*!

Determined to find out what Ms Bumble was buzzing about, she silently scooted closer and listened in.

"At the spelling bee, I will cast my spell," Ms Bumble continued. "I will *hypnotizzzze* the *humanzzz*. They will believe they are my *servantzzz*. From then on, they will do what I command. For I am the evil Queen Bee!"

Queen Bee? Of course! Ellie thought.

That explained the substitute's twitchy hairpins – antennae! It explained her fuzzy black-and-yellow sweater – bee fuzz! And it explained her eyes – real bug eyes!

Ms Bumble was actually Queen Bee, the universe's most royal pest! And if what Ellie had just heard was true, the super-villain had an evil plan. She was going to turn the school into her collection of mindless followers.

"I need to warn Hannah," Ellie said under her breath. A hornet did not make a good friend, and neither did a super-villain's sidekick.

Fast as a lightning bolt, Ellie zigzagged out of the library. The whole class was abuzz when she got back. Everybody got into line, excited to leave for the bee.

At the front of the queue, Hannah was doing some last-second studying. Ellie skidded to a stop next to her friend.

"Um, Hannah?" she said. "I know you're mad at me right now."

Hannah did not look up.

"In fact, I'm sure you'd rather talk to a man-eating meatloaf."

Hannah still did not look up.

"But I have something important to tell you."

Hannah finally put down her list. "Yes?" she said, her face softening.

Ellie took a deep breath. "Okay, here goes nothing. Ms Bumble isn't really a substitute librarian. She's actually the super-villain Queen Bee. She's plotting to take over the spelling bee. And the school. And probably the world because super-villains *love* trying to take over the world. I think it's in their DNA or something."

"Ms Bumble's a super-villain? That's what you wanted to say?" Hannah's face got all pinchy again. "I thought you were going to wish me luck. Instead, you're making up some crazy story to ruin my spelling fun. I knew it! You *are* jealous!"

Ellie opened her mouth to protest. But before she could say another word, Hannah turned away.

Just then, Miss Little waved at the class. "Let's go, class! It's spelling bee time!"

Amanda, Owen and the rest of the students filed out of the classroom. But Ellie couldn't move. Her feet felt like they were stuck in ooey-gooey honey. In minutes, every kid and grownup at Winkopolis Elementary School would get brainwashed with a capital B!

How could Ellie conquer the queen of all villains? Quickly, she X-rayed the room for a weapon. A rolled-up newspaper? A fly swatter? Bug spray? If only Miss Little had better tools for battling evildoers!

Then Ellie spotted the ultimate weapon for foiling Queen Bee – Fuzzball! Every time Ms Bumble saw the badger puppet, she freaked out.

Maybe it'll throw a spanner into her plan! Ellie thought. She swiped it from the bag and then hurried to catch up with her class.

Dex brushed off puppet fuzz as Ellie landed behind him in line. "Is that your superhero sidekick?"

Ellie's eyes rolled to the ceiling. Evil masterminds were better seen and not heard. She pulled out the Ultra Sound Stoppers and corked her ears tightly.

Before turning up the Villain Volume Control, she glared at Dex. "Mind your own beeswax."

CHAPTER 8

ZZZZ

The *Winkopolis Elementary School: Home of the Badgers!* banner greeted everyone in the hall. Kids buzzed like busy bees to their seats. Everyone seemed eager for the spelling bee to begin.

Ellie was the only one without ants in her pants. Instead, she felt like a thousand butterflies were in her stomach. Only she knew what Ms Bumble – ahem, Queen Bee – had planned. If she didn't foil the phoney librarian, everybody was a sitting duck. Even Hannah!

Miss Little's class shuffled into the third row. Hannah, Payton and Dex joined the rest of the spellers onstage.

"Good luck!" Miss Little said.

Ellie watched as Hannah went behind the curtain. What evil awaited her? A toxic stinger? A honeycomb tomb? Ellie feared the worst.

But a few minutes later, Hannah walked onstage. She was safe and sound. A paper with the number seven had been attached to her shirt.

"Phew!" Ellie sighed. She settled into her seat. "That was a close one."

Under the banner, the contestants waited nervously. Payton was fidgeting with her headband.

Layla from Mr Washington's class was picking nail polish off her thumb.

Ellie focused on her best friend. Hannah looked like she'd swallowed a radioactive gnat. She sat on the edge of her seat, her fingers twisting nervously. She was probably worried about forgetting the second *n* in *zinnia*.

Mr Cleveland took his place at the podium. "Welcome to the Winkopolis Elementary School Spelling Bee. Spellers, I'm sure you will B-E-E great." He chuckled. "Here's how it works. When I call your name, you will step up and spell the word I give you. If you make a mistake, you'll be out. Are there any questions?"

The room stayed silent, but a question buzzed in Ellie's brain. Where was Queen Bee? There was no sign of the super-villain anywhere!

Maybe she buzzed off, Ellie thought hopefully. Still, she kept her eyes peeled. Evildoers always struck when you least expected. They were sneaky like that.

"First up, Ian Chang," Mr Cleveland announced.

Ian slid off his chair. He dragged his feet into the spotlight.

Mr Cleveland held up the word list. "Please spell *zone*."

Ian thought for a quiet moment. Then he slowly leaned towards the microphone. His voice boomed across the hall. "Z-O-N-E. *Zone*."

"Correct," Mr Cleveland replied. Ian punched the air proudly and sat down.

Ellie breathed a sigh of relief. No honey oozed down the aisles. No bees swarmed into the audience. So far, the spelling bee was villain-free.

"Dex Diggs."

Ellie sighed. Well, almost villain-free.

Dex smirked as he strutted into position. He planted himself front and centre.

"Spell *zebrafish*."

"*Zebrafish*," Dex repeated. "Z-E-B-R-A-F-I-S-H. *Zebrafish*." Then he spotted Ellie in the crowd. He blew up his cheeks and made a pufferfish face.

Ellie just rolled her eyes.

Next up was Payton. She spelled the word *zapper* correctly. Then it was Hannah's turn.

Ellie watched as her friend stepped forward. *Please let Hannah get a super-easy word,* she thought, crossing her fingers.

"Spell *zesty*," Mr Cleveland said.

Hannah closed her eyes and took a deep breath. "Z-E-S-T-Y. *Zesty*."

Ellie burst into applause. Hannah had spelled the word right!

Mr Cleveland cleared his throat. "Let's wait to applaud until the round is over," he said.

Ellie's cheeks turned red, and she nodded. Just then, she saw Hannah smile.

Ellie's heart leapt. Maybe Hannah was ready to make up! Hopefully they could fix their friendship before Queen Bee turned their minds into mashed potatoes.

* * *

The round ended, and Ellie's mind was still okay. It had not been mashed, hash-browned or double-baked and sprinkled with bacon bits. Nobody had been hypnotised.

Had Queen Bee abandoned her evil plot? Ellie wondered. She shook her head. That was a crazy thought. Super-villains never gave up.

After Layla spelled *zither,* Miss Little yawned. "Ooh, I'm sleepy," she said.

Ellie was puzzled. She didn't think teachers ever got tired. Before she could blink, Amanda yawned too, followed by the student sitting next to her. One by one, everyone in the audience started yawning.

Ellie glanced around the room. Sure enough, as the students spelled *zinc* to *zinger,* the crowd began to fall asleep!

Owen and Joshua dozed off as Ian spelled *zeroes.* When Dex spelled *zeal,* all of the preschoolers went nighty-night.

After Dex sat down, he curled up and let out a snore. *ZZzz-hGGh-zzZZ.*

Ellie sat there, dazed. Why was everyone drifting into dreamland?

"Spell *zzzz,*" Mr Cleveland mumbled behind the word list, his eyes drooping closed.

Ellie gasped as the headmaster nodded off at the podium.

"It's the *z* words on Ms Bumble's list!" she realised. "Hearing *Zs* is making everybody sleepy!"

Thankfully Ellie had turned up the Villain Volume Control dial on her Ultra Sound Stoppers. They had stopped her from zonking out. Turning down the dial, she listened for Queen Bee.

Bzzz . . . bzzz . . .

The noise was coming from the curtain!

Ellie blinked on her X-ray beams and scanned the curtain carefully. Her gaze passed over a pile of grass skirts and a guitar left over from Hawaiian Day. Floating past a blow-up palm tree, the beams stopped.

"Y-I-K-E-S," Ellie whispered, her eyes widening.

In the glow, a bug-like figure stood. It had antennae and six legs. Two pairs of wings buzzed with delight. A crown sat on its head. It was Queen Bee, her majesty of meanness!

The queen rubbed two of her legs together. "My spelling trance worked!" she said wickedly. "Now *it'zzz* time to say the magic *wordzzz*. Then I'll have human worker *beezzz*!"

CHAPTER 9

Fuzzball

The curtain parted, and Queen Bee took centre stage. Her antennae twitched triumphantly to a symphony of snores and whistling noses.

"*Greetingzzz,*" she droned, fixing her eyes on the slumbering crowd. "I am Queen Bee, and I have come to take over *Winkopolizzz* Elementary School. Here, I will make my kingdom, and you, lucky *humanzzz,* will serve me. First, you must listen to my spell."

From behind her back, Queen Bee pulled out a royal sceptre. It was long and pointy, just like a stinger! She raised the sceptre high.

"A-B-C-D-E-F-G . . . ," she began. "When I count to number three . . . G-F-E-D-C-B-A . . . you will wake up and obey. One, two, th –"

"S-T-O-P!" Ellie stood in the aisle. Her cape rippled under the ceiling fan. "I'm Ellie Ultra, and I'm here to tell you to buzz off!"

Queen Bee's antennae flattened. "I do not take *orderzzz,* especially from a human," she said with a sneer.

Ellie didn't move. She had a secret weapon – Fuzzball! "Oh, yeah?" she said, reaching for the badger puppet. "How about from a ba –"

Her hand was empty.

Fuzzfingers! She had left the puppet back at her seat!

Ellie smiled uneasily and backed away. "Uh, did I say buzz off? I didn't mean that. I meant bees are my favourite. They're like little fuzzy teddy bears . . . with stinging butts."

Seemingly flattered, Queen Bee lowered her sceptre. "Oh, really? Well then, let me introduce you to my *friendzzz* . . ."

Suddenly, Ellie heard a buzzing sound. It started out low and grew louder and louder. She looked up. "BEES!"

A black-and-yellow cloud was rolling into the hall. The whole thing was made of bees – zillions of them!

Queen Bee pointed her sceptre at Ellie. "Attack!" she commanded.

The bees buzzed obediently. Then they swirled into a giant tornado and came barrelling down – straight towards Ellie.

"I'm a sitting duck!" Ellie exclaimed as the bee-nado headed closer. So she did what any smart sitting duck would do – she took off, making herself a moving target.

The bees chased after, hot on her tail feathers. Ellie zipped over the stage. They zipped over the stage. She zoomed under the rafters. They zoomed under the rafters. She zigzagged through a maze of drooling fifth graders. As expected, the bees did that too.

Ellie swerved in time to avoid a bee's stinger. It punched a hole into her cape, dotting the *i* in *Ellie Ultra*. "I hope the Ultra Sewing Machine can fix that!"

Trying every move she could think of, Ellie zipped, zoomed and zigzagged until she was exhausted. But it was no use. The bees stayed on her trail.

Finally she blinked herself invisible and ducked behind a seat to rest. The bees sailed overhead as she tried to come up with a better plan.

If only I had a superhero sidekick who could distract the bees! Ellie thought. Then it hit her. She *did* have a sidekick – a fuzzy one!

Ellie flew past Dex, who was no doubt dreaming up ways to bug her. At her seat, she snapped up the badger puppet. It wasn't a villain-fighting invention for B.R.A.I.N., but it had to stop the bees. Otherwise Ellie was going to become a human pincushion!

She reappeared and faced Queen Bee. "Hold on, your evilness! You might think you're going to rule my school. But you're wrong!"

"*You* are wrong, I'm afraid," the queen snapped back. "Not only will I rule your school, I'll take over *Winkopolizzz*. And after that? The world, of *courzzzz!* *Besidezzz,* who will stop me? A silly superhero?"

"More like a super sidekick!" Ellie held up the badger puppet. "Fuzzball wants your friends to back off!"

"Halt!" Queen Bee ordered.

Centimetres from Ellie, the swarm stopped.

Queen Bee stared at the puppet. But surprisingly, she didn't flinch. Grinning like the evil super-villain she was, she replied, "One badger? I'm not scared of one badger now that I have my army!" She turned to the swarm and batted at least a hundred eyes. "You'll give that beast a buzz cut. Won't you, *Sweetumzzz*?"

Bzzz! Bzzz! BZZZ! The bees roared into a circle. Their razor-sharp stingers sliced the air as they flew faster and faster, turning into a terrible buzz saw.

Ellie hugged Fuzzball closely. Glancing up, she looked for a way out when a sign of hope caught her eye. It read, *Winkopolis Elementary School: Home of the Badgers!*

That was it! Ellie flew up into the air, high above the stage, and directed Queen Bee's attention to the banner.

"You might've only seen Fuzzball!" she shouted. "But this school is full of badgers – it says so right here! They're hunting for food, and I've heard they eat insects like you. If you don't leave, they'll turn you and your army into a bee buffet!"

The bees ground to a standstill. They looked nervously at their queen, who was now shaking like a leaf bug.

Queen Bee dropped her sceptre. "We retreat!" she cried. "You can keep your dreadful school. It isn't fit for my kingdom anyway. *It'zzz* crawling with *badgerzzz* – hairy, horrid *BADGERZZZ!*" She waved to the bees. "Come, my *sweetumzzz*! Back to the hive!"

The super-villain's wings flick-a-flicked, and up she went. She retreated out of the room, the swarm following loyally behind.

Splat! Just like that, Ellie had squashed Queen Bee's plan! Kicking up her feet, she broke into a happy jitterbug.

Too bad nobody else was dancing. The whole school – Mr Cleveland, the preschoolers and even Dex, who was mumbling about his fake hiccupping plot – was fast asleep.

The spelling bee is a real snoozefest, Ellie thought.

There was nothing more B-O-R-I-N-G than sitting in a roomful of sleepyheads. It was time to wake everybody up.

Ellie dashed up to the microphone. "Rise and shine!" she said.

No one budged.

Maybe she wasn't loud enough. Ellie took a deep breath and shouted, "WAAAKE UP!"

Miss Little stirred, then went back to sleep. Joshua and Owen rolled over. Mr Cleveland pulled the word list over his head. Ellie did the same thing when she didn't want to get up for school, only she hid under her blanket.

"Now I know how Mum feels," she muttered.

Ellie had to pull out all the stops. She clapped. She stamped. She strummed a guitar and sang, "Mary Had a Little Cape" at the top of her super lungs.

". . . AND EVERYWHERE THAT MARY WENT, HER CAPE WAS SURE TO FLOOOW," Ellie crooned.

Nobody moved an inchworm. Not even a millipede.

Breaking Queen Bee's spell was impossible! Feeling defeated, Ellie sank into a slump. Her bottom landed on something sharp. "Ouch!" she cried and looked down.

It was the queen's sceptre!

Ellie examined the pointy stick. It made her think of the Troll King's staff from *The Staff and the Spell*. In the comic, Princess Power broke the staff to wake up Sparkle Kingdom. Could snapping the sceptre in two snap everybody out of the trance?

"It's worth a try," Ellie said. She held out the sceptre and flexed her muscle power. "Take that, Queen Bee!"

CRAAACK! The sceptre snapped in half. The sound echoed through the hall.

What followed was almost as bad as the sound of buzzing bees.

"Aaahh," Dex yawned, his eyelids opening drowsily. *"Hiccup.* H-I-C-C-U-P."

CHAPTER 10

Friend-not-fiend

Slowly, the crowd and contestants woke up. They yawned and stretched and waited for the next spelling word as if they hadn't just been brainwashed by a superbug.

Mr Cleveland stretched taller than Rubberband Dude. "Let's see. Where was I?" He looked at the list, which was the same one Miss Little had used during class tryouts.

At the recycling bin, Ellie crumpled up Ms Bumble's list. She'd snatched it from the podium before everyone had woken up. "No more snoozapalooza," she said, throwing away the sleepy *z* words.

Now that everyone was wide awake, the spelling bee breezed by like Butterfly Girl riding a helicopter seed. The students spelled a blur of words. They even spelled Ellie's favourite words: *justice, power* and *hero*.

Ian had to spell *victory*, Ellie's most favourite word ever. "V-I-C-T-E-R-Y," he said.

Mr Cleveland kindly shook his head. "I'm sorry, that's incorrect."

Drat! Ellie thought as Ian sat down. *I would've totally got that right.*

Over the next few rounds, the number of contestants grew smaller. Layla added an extra *l* in *polar*, then went back to picking off her nail polish.

Some second graders mixed up the vowels on *count* and *loaf.*

Then Dex swaggered up to the microphone. He turned to Mr Cleveland and gave him a dark and dirty look.

Ellie had seen that look before. It was the same look villains gave anyone who dared to challenge them. It seemed to say, "Go ahead and try, but you'll never stop me! NEVER!"

Mr Cleveland stood his ground. "Spell *daisy,*" he instructed.

"Bwwha-ha-ha!" Dex laughed. "You want me to spell *daisy*? That's it?" Clearly, he was not impressed with the might of Mr Cleveland's five-letter word. "D-A-I-Z-Y. *Daisy.*"

"Incorrect."

Dex's mouth dropped open in shock, and he punched his palm. "No way!"

"Yes way, I'm afraid," Mr Cleveland said. "Please take a seat, Dex."

Dex gave up and sat back down. He had lost the age-old battle of good versus evil, and he knew it. "You may have won this time, but I'll be back," he muttered.

No one else seemed to hear him, but Ellie's super ears picked up the threat clear across the hall. She rolled her eyes again.

When a fourth grader flubbed his word, it was down to Payton and Hannah.

Payton went first. She had no trouble spelling *stubble,* up until she switched the last two letters. "Aw, so close!" she said.

As she sat back down, Mr Cleveland tapped the list on the podium. "Okay, Hannah! It's your turn. If you spell this word right, you're our spelling bee champion! Are you ready?"

Hannah did not look ready at all. She was stuck to her chair, her hair twisted into nervous knots.

Ellie could tell Hannah was too scared to move. It didn't take a super mind-reader to figure that out. Her nerves had a strong hold on her. Hannah needed a boost. So, like a friend – not a fiend – Ellie shouted, "Good luck, Hannah!"

As Mr Cleveland put a finger to his lips, a smile spread across Hannah's face. She came unglued and stood for her word.

"Spell *friend*," Mr Cleveland said.

Hannah looked at Ellie. After a long pause, she said, "F-R-I-E-N-D. *Friend*."

Ellie erupted out of her seat. "YAAAY!" she cheered. Hannah had spelled the word correctly!

Mr Cleveland clapped. "Well done, Hannah! You are the winner of the Winkopolis Elementary School Spelling Bee. Ms Bumble will present you with the first-place trophy." He looked around for the librarian. "Ms Bumble . . . ? Ms Bumble . . . ?"

Ellie turned to the badger puppet. "What do you think, Fuzzball? Should I tell Mr Cleveland about the real Ms Bumble?" After all, alien blobs invaded the school not too long ago, and the headmaster had understood. Compared to that, a bug queen was nothing.

The puppet stayed quiet.

"That's what I figured," Ellie said. She raised her hand. "Um, Mr Cleveland? Ms Bumble left in a hurry. She seemed as busy as a bee! I don't think we'll be seeing her again anytime soon."

Mr Cleveland's eyebrows pinched together. "In that case, I'll do the honours." He reached behind the podium. Out came the trophy. It was gold and shiny, with a picture of a happy bee on the front. In the middle were the words: *First Place Speller.*

"Here you go, Hannah," the headmaster said. "Congratulations!"

Hannah held up her trophy and beamed happily. The audience cheered loudly. Loudest of all was Ellie. She raced over and met Hannah offstage.

"I'm sorry," Ellie began. "I should've been happy when you got into the spelling bee. I hope you'll accept my apology. And this." She dug into her pocket and pulled out the charm bracelet.

"KitKat!" Hannah squealed. "Twirl-errific!" She hugged Ellie and squeezed the air right out of her.

Ellie caught her breath. *In a contest for World's Strongest Hug, Hannah would totally beat the Bear Hugger.*

Hannah wiggled the bracelet onto her wrist. "I'm sorry too. I was mean to you, even though you helped me study. I should've just laughed off your

super-villain story. Could you imagine? Ms Bumble? An evil insect? That would be crazy!"

"Yep, you could say that again," Ellie said, smiling weakly. "Hey! Do you want to go to the new park after school? The swings are really fast! They're like riding a comet, only not as bumpy."

"Sure," Hannah replied. "You know, even without chasing bad guys and runaway asteroids and doing all that other superhero stuff, you're still super to me. You're a super F-R-I-E-N-D."

Ellie smiled. Her determination to be the Spelling Bee Queen seemed so long ago. Now she was happy just being a *friend*.

GLOSSARY

archenemy someone's main enemy

colossal extremely large

contestant person who takes part in a contest

fiend evil or cruel person

foolproof something that is very simple to use and cannot easily go wrong

radioactive made up of atoms whose nuclei break down, giving off harmful radiation

recital musical performance by a single performer or by a small group of musicians or dancers

sceptre rod or staff carried by a king or queen as a symbol of authority

ABOUT THE AUTHOR

Gina Bellisario is an ordinary grown-up who can do many extraordinary things. She can make things disappear, such as a cheeseburger or a grass stain. She can create a masterpiece out of glitter glue and shoelaces. She can even thwart a messy room with her super cleaning power! Gina lives in Park Ridge, Illinois, not too far from Winkopolis, with her husband and their super kids.

ABOUT THE ILLUSTRATOR

Jessika von Innerebner loves creating – especially when it inspires and empowers others to make the world a better place. She landed her first illustration job at the age of seventeen and hasn't looked back since. Jess is an illustrator who loves humour and heart and has coloured her way through projects with Disney.com, Nickelodeon, Fisher-Price and Atomic Cartoons, to name a few. In her spare moments, Jess can be found long-boarding, yoga-ing, dancing, adventuring to distant lands and laughing with friends. She currently lives in sunny Kelowna, Canada.

TALK ABOUT ELLIE!

1. Hannah accuses Ellie of being jealous when she gets into the spelling bee instead of Ellie. Do you think she was right? Look back through this story and give one or two examples of how Ellie acted jealous.

2. Why does Ellie decide she doesn't need to study for the spelling bee? Do you think she was right to act this way? Talk about your opinion.

3. Dex teases Ellie during the school day. How does Ellie tune him out? Talk about another way Ellie could've handled Dex's teasing.

EXPRESS YOURSELF!

1. Ellie's favourite comic book character is Princess Power. She even dresses up like the superhero princess! Pick your favourite character from this book. Write a paragraph about why you like the character.

2. Ellie loves going to Comic Book Day at Winkopolis Books & Toys. Is there an event in your community that you enjoy? Write a paragraph about the event and why you enjoy it.

3. Winkopolis Elementary School's mascot is a badger. Put your super skills to the test and do some research on badgers – or bees! Then write a two to three paragraph report about what you learned.

CHECK OUT THE REST OF ELLIE'S EXTRAORDINARY ADVENTURES!

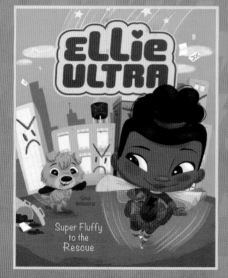

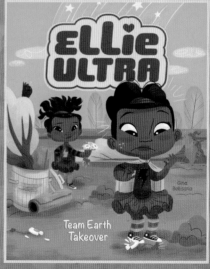